Keoni's Special Gift

Story by Dorinda Lum

Illustrations by Michael Furuya

Mutual Publishing

Acknowledgments

Erin Furuya, Eric Lum, Cesceli Nakamura,
Esme Infante Nii, Margaret South, and Gail Woliver

ISBN-10: 1-56647-915-0
ISBN-13: 978-1-56647-915-8

Library of Congress Cataloging-in-Publication Data

Lum, Dorinda.
  Keoni's special gift / story by Dorinda Lum ; illustrations by Michael Furuya.
     p. cm.
  Summary: Keoni, a little freshwater fish, dreams of flying and gets his chance when his owl friend, Pueo, gives him a magic apple with a warning that he must return by sunset, and a reminder to appreciate what he already has.
  ISBN 1-56647-915-0 (hardcover : alk. paper)
  [1. Contentment--Fiction. 2. Fishes--Fiction. 3. Owls--Fiction. 4. Flight--Fiction. 5. Magic--Fiction. 6. Hawaii--Fiction.] I. Furuya, Michael, ill. II. Title.
  PZ7.L978704Keo 2009
  [E]--dc22

                                        2009029233

Design by Jane Gillespie
First Printing, October 2009

Mutual Publishing, LLC
1215 Center Street, Suite 210
Honolulu, Hawai'i 96816
Ph: (808) 732-1709 / Fax: (808) 734-4094
e-mail: info@mutualpublishing.com / www.mutualpublishing.com
Printed in China

Keoni the ʻoʻopu awoke as he did every day to see the same old sunrise shining down on his familiar stream, high in the mountains.

As he looked down into the valley, he saw birds flying through the rays of sunlight. Keoni sighed, "That sure looks like fun. I wish I could fly."

Keoni's thoughts of flying were interrupted by the sound of his three best friends.

"Good morning," said little ʻŌpae, the shrimp.

"Are you ready for our game of tag?" asked Koloa, the Hawaiian duck.

"What's taking you so long?" Pueo, the wise owl, asked.

"I'm bored with tag," Keoni replied.

Just then, 'I'iwi flew overhead, high above the treetops.
"I wonder what he can see from way up there. I wish I could fly too!" sighed Keoni.

"You're not a bird, you're a fish!" said little 'Ōpae.
"What's wrong with being a fish?" asked Koloa.
"Keoni, if you would like to see beyond the trees,
I have a special gift for you," said Pueo.
"What is it?" Keoni asked excitedly.

Pueo lifted a wing and revealed the most beautiful mountain apple Keoni had ever seen. He dropped it into the water near Keoni and sang,

"Eat this apple and wings shall appear,
Fly like a bird away from here,
Fly over the mountains, follow the sun,
Return to the stream when day is done."

"Mahalo!" said Keoni. He swam up to the apple, took a bite, and suddenly his fins grew into wings.

"I can fly!" Keoni shouted.

"Enjoy your wings, but learn to appreciate what you already have," said the wise owl. "Be sure to come home before sunset or your wings will disappear and you will be lost."

"I will!" answered Keoni. He flapped his magic wings and soared higher and higher above the tallest 'ōhi'a trees. With a gentle nudge from the tradewinds, he was off on his adventures.

Keoni flew down to the sea.
"Surf's up!" he cried as he
jumped onto a surfer's board.

Keoni flew through a little old
plantation town.
"That looks just like the rainbow
in my valley."

Keoni flew to the zoo.
"Amazing! I've never seen anyone like
this before!"

He rested on a rock in the middle of a pond. Suddenly the rock shook. Two large eyes glared at him.

"Oh, you're not a rock at all!" Keoni exclaimed.

"Of course not!" boomed the large creature. "I'm a hippopotamus, and you are interrupting my afternoon nap!"

"I'm sorry, sir," replied Keoni. "I'll be on my way."

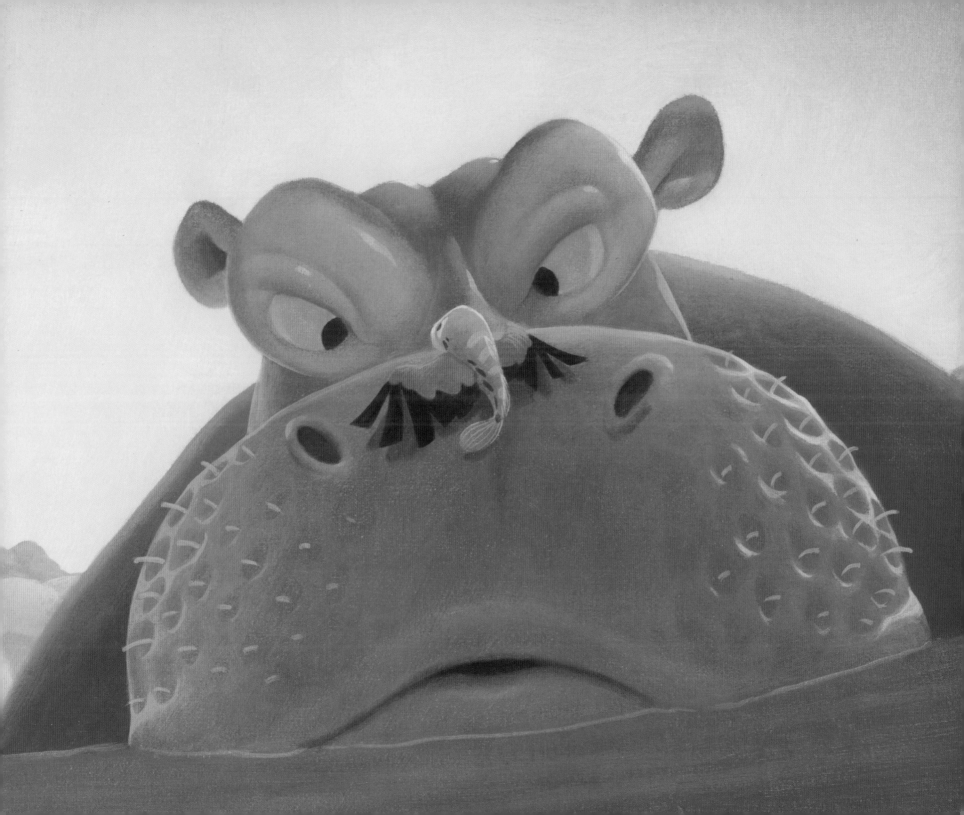

Keoni flew to the tidepools.
"This is so much fun! I could stay here all day!"
But then he heard a desperate-sounding call
in the distance.

"Help!" cried a little voice. "I can't get out!"
Keoni flew over to find a frightened little fish trapped
in a paper cup. He pushed the cup with all his might.

Splash! The cup, the fish, and Keoni fell into the ocean.
"Thank you!" exclaimed the grateful fish as he swam away.

Happy to have helped a friend in need, Keoni began to have thoughts of home. He flapped and flapped but couldn't fly out of the water. His wings were soaked.

Exhausted and afraid, he watched the sun disappear over the horizon.

Keoni knew he had stayed too long. His wings had turned back into fins.

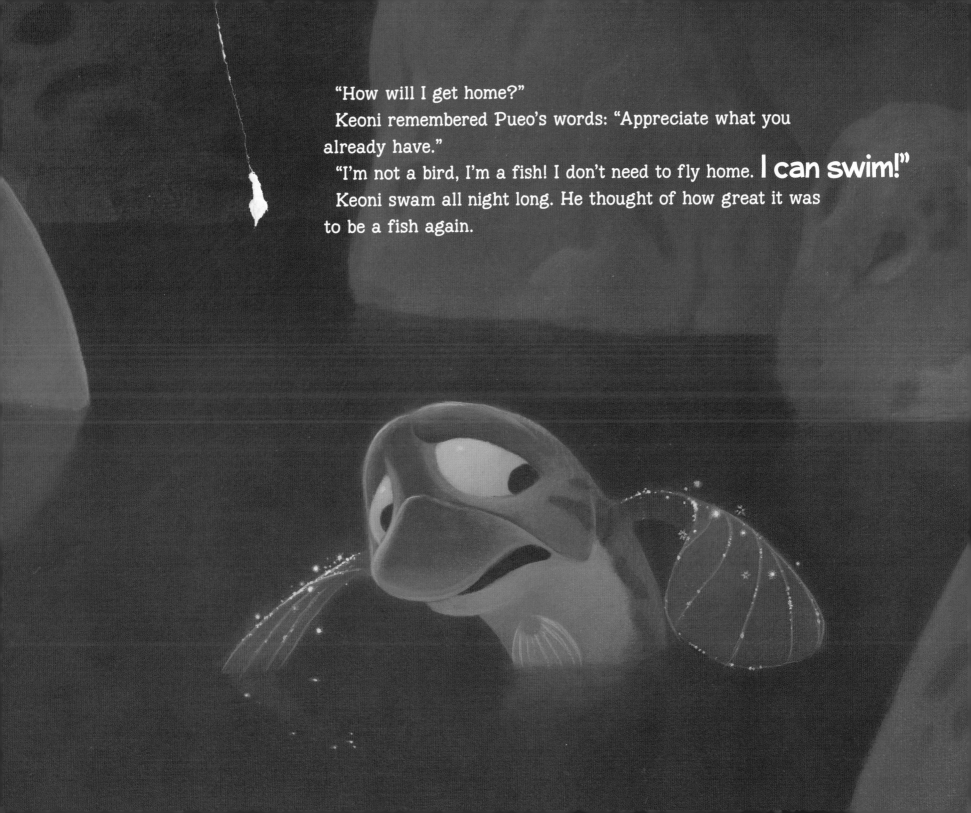

"How will I get home?"

Keoni remembered Pueo's words: "Appreciate what you already have."

"I'm not a bird, I'm a fish! I don't need to fly home. **I can swim!**"

Keoni swam all night long. He thought of how great it was to be a fish again.

Keoni awoke to the sound of familiar voices.
"There you are," said little 'Ōpae.
"Where have you been?" asked Koloa.
"How was your adventure?" Pueo asked.
Keoni told them about all he had seen.

"Thank you for my special gift, Pueo."
"Do you still want to fly like 'I'iwi?" Pueo asked Keoni.
Keoni answered with a huge smile on his face, "I'm not a bird, I'm a fish! Let's play tag!"

About the Author

Dorinda Lum graduated from the University of Hawaiʻi with a Bachelor of Fine Arts in Visual Design, Master of Secondary Art Education, and Master of Education Administration. She is a retired art teacher and administrator with the Hawaiʻi Department of Education and an Artist in the School teaching drawing, painting, and ceramics. In her spare time, she enjoys creating and designing ceramic jewelry and pottery for her label Ceramic Originals by Dorinda.

About the Illustrator

Michael Furuya is the illustrator of the award-winning books *How the B-52 Cockroach Learned to Fly* and *Wailana the Waterbug,* and regional bestsellers *The Adventures of Gary and Harry: A Tale of Two Turtles, Beyond ʻŌhiʻa Valley: Adventures in a Hawaiian Rainforest,* and *A Christmas Gift of Aloha.* Michael attended the California College of Arts and Crafts and graduated with a B.F.A. in Illustration from the Academy of Art College. He lives in Kāneʻohe, Hawaiʻi with his wife Erin and sons Aidan and Brady.